MOPI

IS HAPPY

Written by
JANE ASHER

Illustrated by
GERALD SCARFE

Positive Press

For Iggy
- may you have a wonderfully
multi-coloured life.

Published 2005, Re printed 2009 by:
Positive Press Ltd
28A Gloucester Road
Trowbridge
BA14 0AA
Telephone: 01225 719204
Email: positivepress@jennymosley.co.uk

© Jane Asher
Text by Jane Asher
Illustrations by Gerald Scarfe

ISBN 9-780954058586

Printed by:
Heron Asian Print Ltd
White Hays North
West Wilts Trading Estate
Westbury
Wiltshire BA13 4JT
www.heron-asian-print.co.uk

David was lying in bed one evening thinking. It had been a terrible day. His mum and dad had been busy and his friends never wanted to come over and play with him. Life was really boring and now he counldn't go to sleep.

Then, as he lay watching the shadows on the ceiling, he heard a strange whizzing noise, and he thought he saw something bright green flash down past his window.

"Am I dreaming?" David wondered.

He put one foot out of bed and onto the floor. It felt very cold.

"Well, I'am certainly awake," he said out loud. "And I'm going to go outside and find out what that was."

It was very dark outside and David felt a bit scared.

He was sure he had seen something
but there wasn't anything

on the swing

or behind the tree

or in the old flower-pot.

Then he heard a rustling noise coming from the watering can. He plucked up courage.

"Who's there?" he shouted bravely.

"Nobody," answered a squeaky voice.

David thought for a moment. "You must be somebody or you couldn't talk," he said.

Then he saw something green leap out of the can and disappear behind the bushes.

"Where have you gone?" asked David.

"Nowhere," answered the squeaky voice.

"You must be somewhere," said David.

"Why don't you come out?"

The green thing darted out and leapt at
the washing line.

"Who are you?" said David.

"Can't you see?" it answered. "I'm a shirt."

"No you're not. Don't be so silly," said
David, who was getting a bit cross by now.

"Come down here and tell me who you
really are."

The green creature let go of the washing line and landed at David's feet.

"My name is Moppy," it said. "I jumped down from a star very high up in space. I don't know what to do now."

"Perhaps you'd like to come and stay with me for a bit," said David. "You don't bite or anything, do you?"

"Only food," answered Moppy. And I'd love to stay. You seem very friendly."

David looked worried. "The only trouble is, I'm not sure how Mum and Dad will feel about it. Perhaps I'd better hide you."

Moppy and David walked across the garden towards the house.

"Did you really jump all the way from space?" asked David.

"Oh yes," said Moppy. "I often do that."

They peeped in at the sitting-room window.

"Look," said Moppy. "There are two funny people in there looking at a square box."

"That's Mum and Dad watching television, stupid," whispered David. "Come on!"

David and Moppy crept into the house, quietly shutting the door behind them, and started to go upstairs.

At that moment David's father came out of the sitting-room. David and Moppy ran to hide behing the grandfather clock.

"Who's there?" said Mr Jones.

"NOBODY!" shouted Moppy and David together, and then they both started to giggle.

"Come on, David, I know it's you," said Mr Jones. "What are you doing out of bed and which of your friends is with you?"

David came out from behing the clock.

"Come on, Moppy," he said. "It's no use hiding any longer."

"What on earth is that?" shrieked Mrs Jones, who was watching from the sitting-room doorway.

"He's a green creature who jumped
from space and he's my friend," said
David. "Oh please, please let him stay
here," he begged.

"I'll look after him. He won't be any
trouble."

"Oh yes, David,"
said Mrs Jones. "Just like
you take care of the goldfish,
I suppose. Just look at his
dirty tank."

"It's all right, Mrs Jones,"
said Moppy. "I can look
after myself. And as a matter
of fact I'm also rather good
at cleaning out goldfish."

"Perhaps you can stay
then," laughed Mrs Jones.
"You might even help keep
David clean too. He always
seems to be covered in mud.
Yes, you can stay and sleep
in David's room."

Suddenly something very strange happened.

Moppy's toes turned yellow.

The next moment
his arms did too,

then his legs,

and then his tummy and face until he was
completely yellow all over.

"How extraordinary!" said Mrs Jones.

"It's because I'm happy," said Moppy.

"Sometimes I change colour when I feel things."

"I'm happy too," said David, and he looked down to see whether his toes had turned yellow, but they hadn't. He smiled at his mum and dad, then turned and picked up the bright yellow Moppy.

Halfway up the stairs he stopped, and whispered in Moppy's ear, "I'll be your best friend if you like. I wonder what colour you'll turn tomorrow."

"I wonder," thought Moppy, as David tucked him under his arm and took him upstairs to bed.

Collect the whole series and get to know Moppy in all his moods

**Moppy is Angry
(ISBN 9-7809540585-9-3)**

**Moppy is Happy
(ISBN 9-7809540585-8-6)**

**Moppy is Calm
(ISBN 9-78190486660-8-4)**

**Moppy is Sad
(ISBN 9-7819048660-7-7)**

For more information or to order contact:
Positive Press Ltd, Jenny Mosley Consultancies,
28a Gloucester Road, Trowbridge, Wiltshire BA14 OAA
Tel: 01225 719204 Fax: 01225 712187 E-mail: positivepress@jennymosley.co.uk
Website: www.circle-time.co.uk
Poster sets are also available from Positive Press.

Poster sets also available from Positive Press